W9-DAN-937

THE INVINCIBLE IRON MAN VS CRIMSON DYNAMO

Based on the Marvel comic book series **The Invincible Iron Man**
Adapted by **Steve Behling**
Interior Illustrated by **Craig Rousseau**
and **Hi-Fi Design**
Cover Illustrated by
Mike Norton
and **Brian Miller**

Published by Marvel Press, an imprint of Disney Book Group. No part of this book may be reproduced or transmitted in any form or by any means, electronic or mechanical, including photocopying, recording, or by any information storage and retrieval system, without written permission from the publisher.

For information address Marvel Press, 114 Fifth Avenue, New York, New York 10011-5690.
Printed in the United States of America
First Edition
1 3 5 7 9 10 8 6 4 2
G658-7729-4-12197
ISBN 978-1-4231-4288-1

marvelkids.com

New York

"You call that thing a *dinosaur*?" said Happy Hogan. Happy was talking to his boss, **Tony Stark**. Tony was a brilliant inventor who ran his own company.

"Not a dinosaur," said Tony. "**The Dyna-Soar!** A new spacecraft that will carry astronauts to the Stark Space Station and back. Today is the first test!"

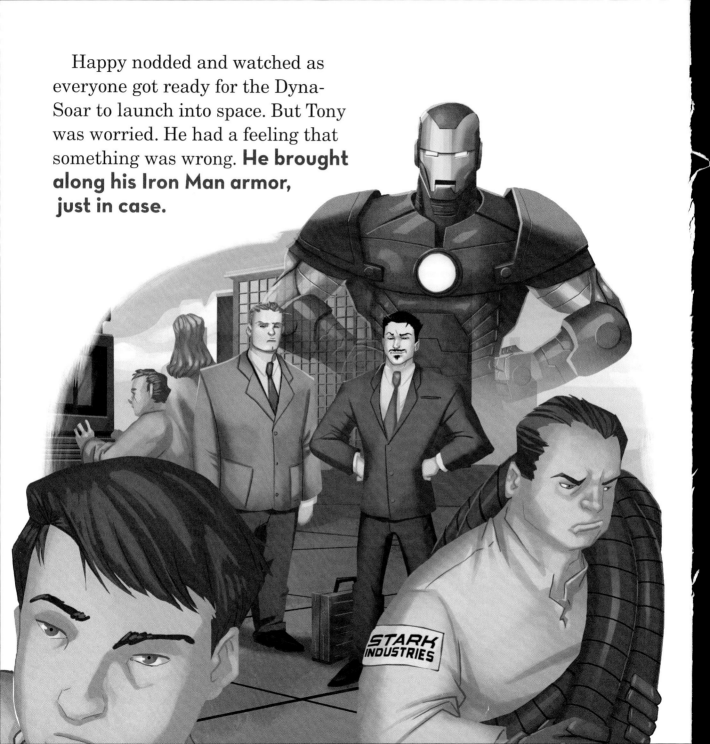

Happy nodded and watched as everyone got ready for the Dyna-Soar to launch into space. But Tony was worried. He had a feeling that something was wrong. **He brought along his Iron Man armor, just in case.**

And something *was* wrong. While Tony and Happy awaited the test, a sinister figure lurked behind them. He looked like one of the technicians, **but he was not. . . .**

Ivan Vanko was no friend of Tony Stark's. He was a scientist, but he did not want to help people. He took his orders from a **mysterious man** from far away.

"Stark's Dyna-Soar test must not succeed," said the mysterious man. **"You must destroy it, Vanko!"**

Meanwhile, the Dyna-Soar was almost ready for launch! The **mighty engines** began to roar, and Tony watched with excitement.

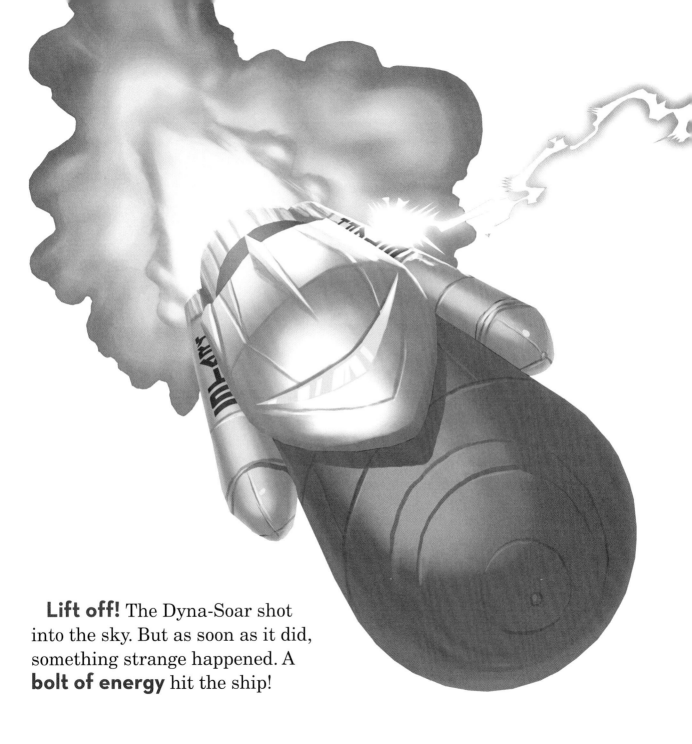

Lift off! The Dyna-Soar shot into the sky. But as soon as it did, something strange happened. A **bolt of energy** hit the ship!

Tony knew that the astronauts inside were in **danger.**

He slipped away so
he could change into his
Iron Man armor.

With his **powerful boot jets,** Iron
Man quickly caught up to the spacecraft.

Soon, he started to get control of the ship. But it took all his strength, and his armor's power supply was getting **lower and lower!**

The Dyna-Soar shot down to Earth like a meteor. Iron Man used nearly **all his energy** to save the astronauts! His armor had very little power left.

But before Iron Man could do anything else, he found himself under attack! "Face your doom," said the strange armored figure. **"Face the Crimson Dynamo!"**

The Crimson Dynamo's blast **hurt** Iron Man. The Armored Avenger fired his **repulsor rays** at his foe, but they did not do anything!

LOW POWER WARNING

Iron Man watched the Crimson Dynamo come closer.
But Tony was more alarmed when he saw that his
armor was nearly out of power! How could he stop
someone as strong as the Crimson Dynamo?

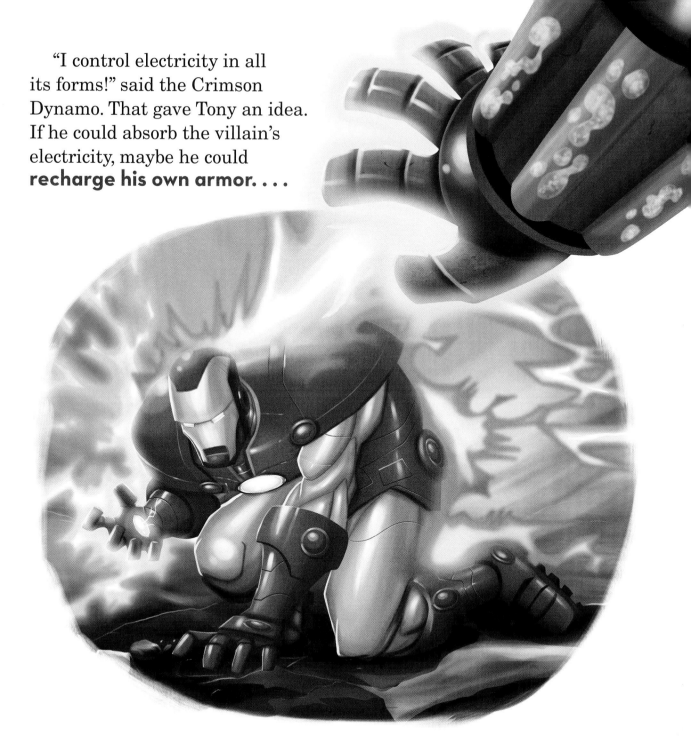

"I control electricity in all its forms!" said the Crimson Dynamo. That gave Tony an idea. If he could absorb the villain's electricity, maybe he could **recharge his own armor. . . .**

Tony made a change to his repulsor rays. Suddenly, the Crimson Dynamo **unleashed all his power.**

Unknown to the Crimson Dynamo, Tony
was **absorbing energy!** With every blast,
Iron Man was growing stronger.

Iron Man grew so strong that he had enough power to **stop the Crimson Dynamo** and send him soaring into the sky!

Against all odds, **Iron Man saved the day!** The villian
had been defeated and the astronauts were saved.